THIS WAI
BELON

First published in *Fairy Tales* 2000 by Walker Books Ltd
87 Vauxhall Walk, London SE11 5HJ

This edition published 2010

2 4 6 8 10 9 7 5 3 1

Text © 2000 Berlie Doherty
Illustrations © 2000 Jane Ray

This book has been typeset in Palatino

Printed in China

British Library Cataloguing in Publication Data:
a catalogue record for this book is available from the British Library

ISBN 978-1-4063-2977-3

www.walker.co.uk

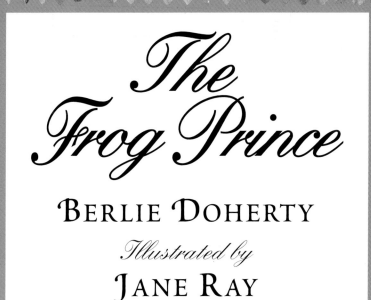

The Frog Prince

BERLIE DOHERTY

Illustrated by

JANE RAY

WALKER BOOKS
AND SUBSIDIARIES
LONDON · BOSTON · SYDNEY

On a perfect day a beautiful young princess was playing in her rose garden with a golden ball. It was her favourite toy, and she sang as she threw it high in the air and watched how it gleamed in the sky, just like the sun. She caught it and bounced it, threw it and caught it, bounced it and threw it. All of

a sudden it slipped out of her fingers, bounced once, and dropped inside a well.

"My ball!" the princess sobbed. "My lovely golden ball!" She ran to the well and peered in, hoping that she would be able to lean down and pick out the ball, but the water in the well was so deep that she couldn't even see the bottom of it, only the reflection of the sky and her own face looking up at her.

"I'd give anything to have my ball back," the princess said aloud. "I'd give away all my jewels and all my fine silk dresses, if only I could have it back."

As soon as she said that a frog hopped

on to the side of the well. He sat dripping just next to the princess's hand, and gazed at her with bulging yellow eyes. "I can help you," he croaked.

"You!" The princess moved her hand away from him quickly. "How can a horrible slimy thing like you do anything to help?"

"I can help get your ball for you, if you promise I can live in your house and eat from your plate and sleep with you in your bed."

"Well, that's not much to promise a silly little frog," the princess laughed, "so I'll say yes!"

And straight away the frog dived into

the well, and down and down into the deep dark water, and soon he swam up with the golden ball in his mouth. He rolled it on to the grass and then the princess picked it up and ran home to her castle, bouncing the ball and singing with joy. In the distance she could hear the frog croaking a strange little song, but she tried not to listen to the words.

This is what he sang, as he watched the princess running away from him.

"Remember the frog
and the words that were said,
Down by the well where the red roses grow;
Your house, and your plate,
and your snowy-white bed,
For you are my love and my lady-o."

But the princess sang louder, to drown out his words.

"What do I care for your silly song!
You can wait for me all day long,
I'll never go back where the red roses grow
And I'll never be your lady-o."

That's what she thought.

That night the princess and her father were just sitting down to the table to eat in the lofty hall of their castle when they heard a rat-tat tat, rat tat-a-tat on the great wooden door. The servant opened the door and there on the threshold sat the frog, dripping. The princess put her hand to her mouth and turned her head away quickly. The frog began to sing, and she put her hands over her ears.

"Remember the frog
    and the words that were said,
Down by the well where the red roses grow;
Your house, and your plate,
    and your snowy-white bed,
For you are my love and my lady-o."

"What does this mean?" her father asked.

So the princess told him how she had lost her favourite golden ball down the well, and how the frog had said he would bring it back to her if she agreed to let him come into her house and eat from her plate and sleep with her in her bed.

"And did you agree?" her father asked.

The princess nodded. "Yes," she whispered, and lowered her head. "But I didn't think he meant it."

And all this time the frog was watching her with his bulging yellow eyes, and gulping and dripping on the threshold.

"Well," her father said. "A promise is a promise. You must ask your frog into the house."

So the princess went to the door and invited the frog to come in, and when she sat down again to her meal he hopped up on to the table beside her, and ate from the side of her plate.

"He is disgusting!" the princess said, but her father said nothing. When it was time for her to go to bed the princess stood up and the frog hopped a little closer to her and blinked slowly.

"Oh!" she shuddered. "Do I have to take him with me?"

"You made a promise," her father reminded her.

So the princess picked up her candle in one hand and the frog in the other and climbed up the long twisty stairs, to her room. She held the frog well away from her, and in the light of the candle his legs dangled long thin shadows, and his eyes gleamed like deep round wells.

When she woke up the next morning, the frog had gone. "Thank goodness!" the princess said. "Now I can forget all about him."

Next evening, when the princess and her father were just sitting down to their meal there came a rapping at the door, rat-tat-a-tat! and there was the frog, gulping and dripping and slimy, watching her with his bulging yellow eyes.

"Remember the frog
    and the words that were said,
Down by the well where the red roses grow;
Your house, and your plate,
    and your snowy-white bed,
For you are my love and my lady-o."

"A promise is a promise," her father said.

"But he's so disgusting! Oh, he's horrible! Oh, how I hate frogs!"

The princess invited the frog into her house and when she sat down he jumped up and ate from the plate, and when she went to her bed he slept with her on her snow-white sheets. But when morning came, he had gone.

"But he will come tonight, I know it," the princess said. "He'll come every day of my life and I'll never get rid of him."

"That's as may be," said her father. "But a promise is a promise."

And sure enough, the frog came at the end of the day, and sang his song in the doorway.

"*Remember the frog*
 and the words that were said,
Down by the well where the red roses grow;
Your house, and your plate,
 and your snowy-white bed,
For you are my love and my lady-o."

He blinked his watery eyes at her, and sat on her plate gulping her food when she ate, and jumped into the palm of her hand when she stood up to go to her bed. She kissed her father goodnight and went sadly up to her room, and put the frog on to her snowy-white pillow, and she sang to him.

"What do I care for your silly song!
You can wait for me all day long,
I'll never go back where the red roses grow
And I'll never be your lady-o."

The frog just gazed at her, and gulped, and blinked.

And that night the princess dreamed of the deep dark well, and the red roses that trailed over its mossy walls, and woke up to such a strong scent of roses that she thought for a moment she was in the garden.

She lay in her bed half awake and half asleep, watching the sun as it rose in the sky like a golden ball.

"Princess," said a quiet voice, and she sat up startled. Standing by her bed was a young man with bright, smiling eyes.

"Who are you?" the princess asked.

"The frog," he said. "The frog prince."

He took her hand in his and told her that he had been enchanted by a wicked magician who had turned him into a frog and thrown him down the deepest well.

"I watched you every time you came into your garden, and I loved you – but oh! how hopeless it was! You were a princess and I was a frog! But when you let me

come into your house and eat from your plate and sleep with you in your bed, you broke the magician's spell. You kept your promise, and that's more powerful than anything a magician can do. You turned me back into a prince."

"I like you much better now you're not a frog," the princess said.

"And I never want to leave you." He took her other hand in his. "I would like to be with you every day of my life, for you are my love and my lady-o."

The princess couldn't help smiling. "Does that mean you want to marry me?" she asked.

"It does," said the frog prince. "Will you?"

And the princess said *yes*.

Titles in the Fairy Tale Series

Available from all good bookstores

www.walker.co.uk

For the best children's books, look for the bear.